Prairie Dog Town

JANETTE OKE'S

Animal Friends

Prairie Dog Town

Illustrated by Nancy Munger

BETHANY BACKYARD®

Prairie Dog Town
Revised, full-color edition 2001
Copyright © 1988, 2001
Janette Oke

Illustrations by Nancy Munger
Design by Jennifer Parker

Published by Bethany House Publishers
11400 Hampshire Avenue South
Bloomington, Minnesota 55438
www.bethanyhouse.com

Bethany House Publishers is a Division of
Baker Book House Company, Grand Rapids, Michigan.

Printed in China

Library of Congress Cataloging-in-Publication Data

Oke, Janette
  Prairie dog town / by Janette Oke ; illustrated by Nancy Munger.—
Rev., full-color ed.
      p. cm. — (Janette Oke's animal friends)
Summary: Flick, a curious young prairie dog, learns about the pleasures and dangers of life outside his family's underground home, as well as the importance of obeying his parents.
  ISBN 0-7642-2455-7 (pbk.)
  [1. Prairie dogs—Fiction. 2. Animals—Infancy—Fiction. 3. Conduct of life—Fiction.] I. Munger, Nancy, ill. II. Title.
  PZ7.O4114 Pr 2001
  [E]—dc21
                                                              00-012200

Dedicated with love to the children
of our Sunday school class at
St. Mark Missionary Church.
May God richly bless you.

JANETTE OKE was born in Champion, Alberta, during the depression years, to a Canadian prairie farmer and his wife. She is a graduate of Mountain View Bible College in Didsbury, Alberta, where she met her husband, Edward. Both Janette and Edward have been active in their local church as Sunday school teachers and board members. The Okes have four grown children and several grandchildren and make their home near Calgary, Alberta.

CHAPTER
One

I rolled my eyes and sighed. How would I ever remember all of the things that Mother was saying? She had already been talking for what seemed like hours. And my brother and sisters and I *had* to know all of the instructions that she was giving us.

We'd never remember. *I'd* never remember.

"And remember," Mother added. "Whenever you hear the signal, stop what you are doing and don't move. Don't even blink your eyes. If the signal comes a second time, run home as fast as you can. Just run!"

"What if we don't hear a second

signal?" someone asked.

It was Annabelle. She *would* ask questions. She was Mother's pet. She always sat and listened and made the rest of us look bad.

"If there is not a second signal, then you may go right on eating," Mother told her.

"How long should we wait?" asked Annabelle.

"Count slowly to ten," said Mother.

I hoped that she was finally going to let us go outside, but she didn't. She kept talking.

"Our town is a nice place to live, with many friends and neighbors. Everything that you need is right here. But you must remember the rules. All of the town is divided into territories. No one comes on our territory, and we do not walk on the territory of another. That is the only way to live in peace with the neighbors. Is that clear?"

We all nodded.

"Your father and I are very strict about the rules," went on Mother. "We don't ever want to hear a report that our children are careless about following them."

"No, Mother," we said in unison.

I thought that we were never going to be able to escape Mother and get a look at the big world. It was all that I could do to hold myself still.

CHAPTER
Two

"Now," said Mother. "Your father is waiting outside. He has gone out to check if it is safe for your first trip up."

What would it be like? Would it be as exciting as it sounded when Mother and Father spoke of the outside world? Was it really as big as they said? Were there really others like us, all around us as far as my eye could see?

"Now, let's line up," Mother was saying. "Annabelle, you follow me. Frisk, you follow Annabelle. Then Louisa and Sue Mary. Flick, you bring up the rear."

I groaned. Why should I be the last one to see the outside world? Why should

everyone, even Annabelle, get to go first?

We inched forward slightly. Then came the whisper, "Annabelle is listening now." I wished that I were closer so I could give Annabelle the nudge that would send her out into the new world.

We stopped while Frisk took his turn, and then we moved on again. Frisk hadn't taken nearly as long as Annabelle. Louisa was next. By the time that she moved up, I could see daylight.

I could hardly stand it. I wanted to push everyone aside and rush out.

Louisa finally went out, and then it was Sue Mary's turn.

"Oh, Flick," she whispered. "It's beautiful! So big! So—"

"I'd like to see it for myself," I said. "Please!"

She moved aside then.

I tried. I mean, I really tried. I did stop—
sort of. I did tilt my head to listen, first one
way and then the other. And I did take one
big long sniff. Then I poked my head out of
the entrance and looked at the world
beyond our tunnel.

CHAPTER
Three

For a minute I saw nothing. The brightness of the sun had blinded me. I blinked and blinked, trying to focus. Then slowly I could see shapes and movement. The world just went on and on and on. I'd had no idea that it was so big.

"Isn't it great?" whispered Sue Mary, and I pushed my way up to sit beside her.

"Did you spot the sentries?" came Mother's stern voice.

I looked around me then. Over to my right was a large prairie dog with sharp black eyes and a stub of a tail. He stood on his hind legs, his eyes darting back and forth over the whole area before him. Now and then he tilted his head and looked toward the sky. As I watched, he shifted his body so that he could look to his right.

"Him?" I asked Mother.

"That's one," Mother replied. "I want you to find at least three of them."

I turned in the other direction and spotted another one.

"Him?" I asked Mother.

She nodded. "One more."

Sue Mary nudged me and nodded her head just slightly in the direction that lay directly ahead of us. I looked that way, and sure enough, standing on a rock was a third sentry. He was a little lighter in color than the other two, and he blended in with the rock perfectly.

"Three," I pointed out to Mother.

She nodded her head and began to walk. "Your father has found a nice patch of grass off this way," she said. "Come, we'll show you what is good eating."

I was a bit impatient with that. I wasn't that hungry, and there was so much to see. I wanted to just look and look.

Mother must have read my mind, for she spoke softly. "After you get more familiar with the area and with the rules, you may go off on your own. But for the next few days, we want you to stay close to the family."

It bothered me. It seemed that I had been waiting forever and ever to get up top and see the amazing world. Now here I was with the world right before me, and I had to stay close to Mother.

I choked back my grumble and followed quietly. Exploring would be allowed later. Mother had promised.

CHAPTER
Four

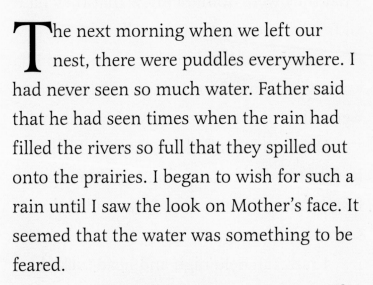

The next morning when we left our nest, there were puddles everywhere. I had never seen so much water. Father said that he had seen times when the rain had filled the rivers so full that they spilled out onto the prairies. I began to wish for such a rain until I saw the look on Mother's face. It seemed that the water was something to be feared.

I was just beginning to enjoy my meal, when a sharp bark came from the nearest sentry. I froze, my foot in the air, my whole body tense. It was the first time that I had heard the warning signal. But Mother had trained us so well that I knew exactly what to do.

It seemed like I stood there forever. I could sense my family members about me, but I didn't dare to even turn my head to see what they were doing. I knew that they had all frozen into position, as well.

Then came another sharp bark, and I knew *that* signal, too. That meant that we were all to dive for the safety of our tunnel.

Without even looking around, I began to run. I hadn't known that I could run so fast, but for some reason, I was suddenly scared to death.

I ran. Tail held high and head tucked down low, I ran. All around me was the patter of other running feet as small bodies scurried to their homes.

Just as I neared our entrance, another sentry gave the cry of alarm. That really frightened me. I tried to run faster.

Suddenly, my feet tripped, and I flipped end over end, sailing through the air and landing on my face. I got up as quickly as I could, shook my head, and headed for the first open door that I saw.

"Halt!" cried an angry voice. "What are you doing here?"

I skidded to a stop, blinking my eyes. I didn't recognize the voice. It wasn't Mother or Father. It was then that my nose began to work again. This was not our tunnel. No wonder it was not Mother's or Father's voice. In my confusion, I had dived into someone else's home by mistake.

"I didn't mean—" I began, but he was getting awfully close to me. And he looked so big and so mad.

"I fell—I was running and I fell. I meant to go home."

"Home? This is my home," the prairie

dog cried.

"I know. I'm sorry. Truly I—"

"Out!" he screamed at me. "Out."

"But...but the...the danger isn't passed."

"Out!" he cried again.

I shut my eyes tight and ran outside again. And then I heard the most welcome sound that I had ever heard. It was Father's voice, and he was calling me. There was Father, standing on his hind legs, calling me to our tunnel.

I ran as fast as I could. I was almost to the entrance when Father suddenly disappeared. All that I saw was a flip of his tail, and he was gone from my view. Then I saw something else. A great shadow passed over me. A big bird with very large wings was swooping toward the earth.

This was one of the enemies that I had

been warned about! This was why the sentries had cried. This was why Father had disappeared with a whisk of his tail. And this was who wanted me for breakfast.

With a final burst of speed, I flung myself forward and tumbled into the opening of our home just as the *whoosh* of wings passed over my head.

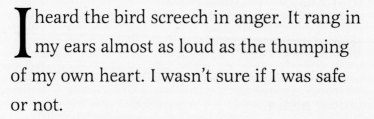

I heard the bird screech in anger. It rang in my ears almost as loud as the thumping of my own heart. I wasn't sure if I was safe or not.

"Are you all right?" Father asked, coming up beside me. I couldn't speak. I couldn't even nod.

Mother pushed forward then. She ran her nose over my cheek and shoulder. Already she had found the tender spot where I had bumped my shoulder on the way in.

"You're hurt," she cried in a worried voice.

"He's fine," said Father. "He's safe.

That's the main thing."

"Come, dear," said Mother. "We need to get away from the entrance. Come."

Mother turned to the others. "That was a close call," she said. "I'm sure you understand now what Father and I have been trying to teach you."

Just thinking about it made me start to shiver again.

"You've learned two very important lessons today," went on Mother. "And I do hope that you never experience them again."

I nodded. I hoped so, too.

"One is that you never, never intrude into someone else's home. No one will treat such an intrusion lightly."

"Why?" asked Frisk. "Why was he so mean? Flick meant no harm. He wasn't even going to stay."

"We all are very protective of our homes," said Father. "Our homes are meant for us—only. We guard them with our lives. We do not want intruders. Our family must be safe here. Other animals could harm our children, steal our food, or—"

"But Flick wasn't gonna do any of those things," cut in Sue Mary. "He just wanted to hide."

"Flick must remember that we check our homes with our sense of smell. We can tell immediately when we enter our tunnel if it has been visited by anyone other than our own family."

I hadn't known that it was *that* important. *That* complicated. I was sorry that it had happened. I hadn't meant to destroy the safety of our neighbors. I hung my head.

"You also learned," went on Mother, "that a hawk's talons are to be feared. I still don't know how you ever made it to safety, Flick. They seldom miss."

She reached over and nuzzled me again, and there were tears in her eyes.

I was quite willing to agree with Mother. I had learned two very important lessons. And like her, I hoped that I never had to experience them again.

CHAPTER
Six

Spring had passed well into summer. The hot, sandy prairie baked in the afternoon sunshine. The prairie animals were growing bigger, and even the baby birds had left their nests. Each day held so many things to see and to learn. I began to get excited again about growing older and being able to explore.

One thing had always puzzled me. At the end of each day, the sun went down and it turned to night. Father said that night was a dangerous time. All of us had to be safely tucked away in our beds before darkness came.

When I asked Father about the night,

he knew very little about it.

"It's black," said Father.

"It's dangerous," added Mother. "It's filled with enemies."

"The hawk?"

"No," said Father.

"The coyote?" I asked.

"I really don't know," Father admitted. "I have never been in the night to find out. But I've heard that there are many creatures that hunt at night. And they aren't looking for prairie grasses, either."

"You mean us?" Sue Mary's eyes got big as she asked the question.

"They would like to find us—yes," said Father. "Only we outsmart them. We go to our beds."

Sue Mary looked afraid. I was sure that *she* wouldn't be checking out the night.

I didn't say any more. I didn't want to

make anyone suspicious.

That night when we went to bed, I made sure that I slept the closest to the tunnel. I didn't want to be crawling over bodies when I sneaked from the bed.

It seemed to take forever for everyone to fall asleep. I was afraid that morning would come before I could peek outside.

At last I heard Father's heavy snores and Mother's even breathing. I eased myself away and crept quietly. The nearer I got to the top, the more excited I became. I could hardly wait to see the outside world at night.

At first I was disappointed. It was so dark without the sun that I could not see anything. I sat at the entrance to our home, blinking and trying to get my eyes to focus better. But my eyes were not made for the darkness.

I did remember my training and checked carefully before leaving the entrance. Now that I was out and free to explore the night world, I wasn't quite sure where to go.

I decided to see what I could find to eat. At night, with no neighbors around, I could eat whatever and wherever I pleased.

"Wouldn't it be wonderful if I found a special snack?" I was telling myself, when all of a sudden I felt a shadow pass over my head.

CHAPTER
Seven

My first instinct was to duck, but I listened for the bark of the sentry. It was then that I reminded myself there *wouldn't be* any sentries. Not a one. They, too, were all sleeping soundly in their beds.

If there weren't any sentries, then who would stand on guard for me as I fed? I had never had to worry about that before.

"I'll be my own sentry," I told myself. "I can watch as well as eat."

But I didn't really do much eating. There was too much to see. I couldn't believe how different the world looked by night.

A slight movement off to my right made me freeze in my tracks. Thankfully, it was only Jack, the large rabbit who also occupied our part of the prairie. I had never really spoken to him before. But to my surprise, he looked my way and nodded.

"Hi," I said shyly.

His whiskers twitched as he nibbled at the grass. He spoke around it. "Hi. How come you're not in bed? I thought prairie dogs sleep at night."

"We do. I mean, well . . . they do. I . . . I couldn't sleep. Didn't want to sleep," I corrected. "When do you sleep?" I asked him.

"Whenever I like. I take naps. Sleep awhile, feed awhile."

It sounded like a good way to do things. I wondered why we didn't do it that way.

Then we would be able to see both day and night.

Jack must have read my mind. "Your eyes aren't made for the night," he said. "You'd never see the enemies coming up behind you."

The way Jack said it made me shiver. I quickly swung my head around to check to be sure that one wasn't sneaking up on me now. I guess I expected to see a tall, dark object ready to pounce.

"What . . . what animals are out at night?" I asked him, thinking that he would know.

"Oh, coyotes, badgers, bobcats . . ."

"Snakes?"

"Yeah, snakes."

Jack had listed a good number of creatures on my enemy list.

"What about hawks?" I went on, as

though it didn't really matter much.

"Most of them feed in the daytime."

"Yeah, I know," I said. "On prairie dogs."

Jack laughed, though I really couldn't see anything so funny about it.

"On rabbits, too," he said. "When they can catch them, that is. Me, I've outrun more than one hawk in my day."

"Outrun them?" I said, doubting his story. "How?" I knew a little about how fast a hawk could swoop.

"Just duck and dodge," said Jack. He swung his shoulders this way and that to demonstrate.

"Well, I hope we won't need to do any ducking and dodging tonight," I said with a husky voice. I wasn't built like a rabbit.

CHAPTER
Eight

J ack took me on a tour all around our
town. The hours went by quickly, and at
last we agreed that I'd better get back to the
nest and get some sleep before morning
came. Already the grass was getting wet
with dew, and my feet were damp.

"I'll see you home," Jack said. I was
about to say that I could find my way just
fine, when the moon dipped behind a cloud
again.

I could hardly see at all. Jack realized
that when I tripped over a rock in my path.

He was hopping along beside me, both
of us giving full attention to where I was
placing my feet, when there was a scurry

behind us. I swung around to stare into the darkness, the fur on my neck standing up in fright. I could see nothing.

Jack must have seen something with his nighttime eyes. He gave me a rough shove and yelled, "Run, Flick! Run!"

I didn't know what I was running from, but I didn't wait to ask. I just made a dash for the entrance to our tunnel and ran as fast as my short legs could take me.

The moon came out again. When I looked back over my shoulder, I saw a huge animal right on my tail. I was sure he was ready to take a bite at me, when suddenly Jack dashed between us.

The animal stopped just long enough for me to gain a bit of ground. Then he changed his mind and was off after Jack in a flash. I could hear them both smashing through the prairie grasses as they made their way across the bumpy ground.

I was still frozen in my tracks, shivering at my close call, when I heard another noise. I didn't stick around to find out what it was. I ran as fast as I could for home.

I tumbled down our tunnel, fighting for breath. My heart was pounding in my chest. All the time that I rushed to safety, I wondered about Jack. That was a brave thing he had done. Was he able to outrun the animal?

I slowed my steps and began to creep as quietly as I could toward the nest and the family. I felt chilled right to the bones, but I wasn't sure if it was from the cold or the fright. I shivered again, aching for the warm bodies of my brother and sisters.

One thing I knew for sure. I'd had my fill of night. Father and Mother were quite right. It was dangerous!

CHAPTER
Nine

I slept in the next morning. I even missed breakfast. By the time I got up and made my way outside to eat, dark clouds covered the sky. Thunder rolled in the distance, too.

I knew that it wouldn't be long before it rained. I hurried off to grab all I could before the storm began to splash around me.

I didn't get much. I ate as long as I dared, then scurried off for home. I did hope that the rain wouldn't last long. I knew that the food

supply in the storage rooms was off limits, except for an emergency. And Father wouldn't think my sleeping in was an emergency.

Some of the family members were still gathered near the entrance when I came in. Mother scolded me about my wetness, then began to dry me off.

I went back to bed grumbling. I had the feeling that my stomach wasn't going to let me get much sleep.

After a while I tried to go out again— then again. But each time that I looked, the rain was still falling.

I thought that I would starve to death before I was able to get back to feeding. Finally, I could stand it no longer. I sneaked from the den and went out to eat.

Everywhere I went there was water. My feet were wet before I took three steps, and

they soon were so cold I could hardly stand it.

My fur got wet, too. The heavy rain continued to beat down upon my back, soaking me right through to the skin.

I ate as fast as I could. The grass was muddy and wet, too, and not very good. But I ate it anyway. Then I hurried toward home, thinking now of the warmth that the snuggling family in the cozy nest would provide me.

"You're soaked to the bone," Mother said when she saw me. "You'll catch your death of cold."

"I'll soon warm up when I get to bed," I told her, trying to head for the bed.

"Oh no, you don't," said Mother, taking a firm stand. "You aren't crawling into bed soaked like that. You'll get the bedding and your family all wet, too."

I looked down at myself. I supposed she was right, but I was freezing. How would I ever warm up if I couldn't go to bed? Where would I sleep?

Mother told me. "You can sleep in the empty storage room," she said. I shivered at the thought. There wasn't even a bed in there.

"Come," she said. "I'll dry you off the best I can."

When she left, I curled up and tried to go to sleep in spite of my shaking body. Mother was soon back. She had brought me some bedding from the nest.

"This might help some," she said as she tucked it about me. "Try to get some sleep."

I tried, but it sure was difficult to do. I was shivering so much that my whole body shook. I wondered just which was worse—being cold or being hungry.

CHAPTER
Ten

I had never seen so much rain in all my life. I thought that the sky was falling down. The clouds kept pouring out water.

It was too wet to go outside to eat, and everyone was getting hungry. Even Father. Finally, he decided that this was an emergency. He took out some of the food from the storage room. It really wasn't enough to fill us up, but at least it took the edge off.

To pass the time, we tried to sleep all we could. That worked for a while, but after a few days, we were just plain bored. Little

arguments kept breaking out over the tiniest things.

Our home had been built with safety in mind. The mound around the entrance was made to keep out the water when rain began to cover the ground around us. But even that wouldn't hold out the water forever. If it kept raining, we might be in trouble.

Father watched as the rain formed huge puddles. He watched more carefully as the puddles made big pools. Soon our whole area was beginning to look like a lake, with the edges of prairie dog homes sticking up through the water.

Father called us together for a meeting. "We're going to seal off the front against the rain. The back entrance is higher. If we need to get out, we'll use the back."

It was hard work, but once we had the

tunnel sealed, Father opened up the back entrance. He didn't want to take any chances if we needed the back door as an escape.

That night, we curled up together and slept as usual. I guess Mother and Father spent the entire night keeping watch on the rain. I don't know if they watched together or took turns, but it seemed that neither of them got much sleep.

I had just gotten up to check on Mother when I heard Father's alarm. Suddenly, we were all running for the back door. I turned back to see what was going on, but all I could see was water. It was coming fast, trying to catch us.

I was sure that we'd never make it. The

cold water was already washing over me. I struggled to stay on my feet. My fur was wet, and I could hear the roar of the water.

Just as I thought that I couldn't possibly hold my breath any longer, my head broke through the water and I could breathe again.

In a few more steps, I had made it outside the back door and was out on the open prairie. At least, it *had* been the open prairie. Now it looked far more like the open sea.

CHAPTER
Eleven

Water was everywhere. I couldn't believe my eyes. Here and there a prairie dog home showed, but mostly everything was washed away.

All around us were shivering families, clinging together for warmth. We were silent, though. We didn't want to alert any of our enemies.

It was still raining. The sky was overcast and looked as if it would keep on raining forever. I shivered at the thought.

There was nothing to do. No place to go. No place to get in out of the rain. We just had to stand right there and let it run down our backs and drip off our noses. I

had never been so miserable in my life.

We couldn't eat, either. All of our roots and grasses were under water. I wondered what we would ever do for dinner.

It was late in the afternoon before the rain finally stopped. But then our real troubles began. As soon as the rain stopped and the clouds rolled away, the hawks were back in the sky again.

As many of us as possible pressed under the overhanging rocks. Others pushed into bushes or mud clumps—anywhere we could find some kind of cover.

Somehow we made it through the day. As the sun went down, the hawks went to roost for the night. I breathed a sigh of relief.

But it was dark now, and I knew all too well what kind of dangers lurked in the dark.

CHAPTER
Twelve

Father and some of the other men were talking about what to do, when I saw Jack. I was very glad to see him.

I guess my relief showed in my face. But I didn't dare say too much with my family around. I knew that they would be asking questions if they saw me talking to the rabbit.

Jack looked at me, and I caught his wink. Then he turned to my father.

"You folks need some help?" he asked.

"I guess we need about all the help we can get," my father said. "But I'm not sure what you can do."

"Well, I can't give you back your home,"

said Jack. "But I know where there is a place that is warm and dry, even though it isn't what you have been used to."

Father nodded. I knew that he just wanted to get us all to a safe place.

"Certainly," responded Father. "Thank you."

"No problem," said Jack, and he began to lead the way.

Jack caught himself going a bit too fast for us every now and then. He'd have to slow down to let us catch up.

When we finally got there, it was just as Jack had said. The place was warm and dry and sheltered from enemies.

It was a hollow

spot under a fallen tree. It looked snug and warm, and I knew that my folks were thankful for it. Still, Mother couldn't help but wrinkle up her nose as she entered. Mother did not care much for the smell of the place.

The home might not have been what we were used to, but we sure were glad to have it. We snuggled close together and tried to forget our empty stomachs. I guess we all slept. I know that I did.

When I woke again, the sun was shining. We all began to stir. And even before any of us had our eyes open, I heard Louisa say, "I'm hungry."

I could have echoed the words. I was starving.

We found when we left the borrowed nest that Jack had done us another favor. We were above the water level. The grass up higher wasn't touched by the water.

Father and Mother took the first shift as sentries. The rest of us lost no time in finding something to eat.

All day long Father kept his eye on the prairie land below us. I knew that both he and Mother were anxious to get back to our own home. It still didn't look very hopeful to me. Besides, I really liked our new place. It was a lot nicer than living underground.

CHAPTER
Thirteen

I t was several days later before Father
decided that it looked dry enough down
below to get on with the clean-up chores.
We all knew that there was a big job ahead
of us. And I was old enough now that I
knew I'd have to share a big part of the load.

We started back down the slope,

Father's eyes on the sky and
Mother's eyes over the
land. I knew that danger
lurked all around us.

When we got home,
we found a disaster. All
around us neighbors were
trying to dig out and repair

their homes. Everything was ruined.

I shuddered as I thought about it and was even more thankful for Jack. I guess Father and Mother were, too. I heard Mother say to Father, "We must remember to do something nice for that kind Jack Rabbit. It was so kind of him to think of us."

"It was," said Father. Then he added slowly, "And curious, too. There were lots of other families that needed help. Why did he pick us?"

"I don't know," said Mother.

Then Mother's eyes turned directly on me. I couldn't help but squirm, but I hoped with all of my heart that she didn't catch on.

We all set to work on our house. It had to be all dug out again. It still felt a bit damp in spots, but Father told us that it would soon dry out. Mother and the girls managed to find some dry bedding, and they began to make our beds again.

Our emergency food supply was the biggest concern. It was hard enough to find grass to fill our hungry tummies now. It was much harder to find extra grass for storing. I knew it would be some time before we felt safe again.

CHAPTER
Fourteen

The weeks went by, and we were slowly getting back on our feet. The grass was back, which meant we spent a lot of time gathering it up and carrying it to our storage room.

One afternoon, I was out looking for grass with Annabelle when I heard the sentry cry. I froze. I couldn't see any shadow overhead, and I hadn't seen any coyote or bobcat lurking about. I thought it was a false alarm.

But suddenly, the second alarm was sounded, and I followed Annabelle and scurried for home. I ducked in just as I had been taught. Father was there waiting at the entrance, taking the family count in Mother's place.

"Where's Mother?" I asked.

"She hasn't come yet," said Father with a worried look on his face.

"What is it?" I asked next.

"A stampede," said Father.

"Stampede?" I had never seen one before. I don't think that I had even heard of one before.

"Cattle," explained Father. "Running cattle."

"Running from what?"

"I don't know," said Father. "They just run. And they run over anything that is in their way."

"Where do they run to?" I asked.

"Who knows," said Father. "They just run until they stop. I don't think that they are going anywhere."

There was a rumbling sound that was getting much closer now. I was starting to get scared, and I guess Father was, too. I wanted to ask if I could go out searching for Mother. But I knew Father would never let me.

Just then, there was the worst noise I had ever heard. Hundreds of trampling, traveling feet began to pound away at the prairie earth above our heads. Dust came down the tunnel and started me coughing. Father was coughing, too.

"We'd better get down," he said. "Mother won't come now."

"I'll be down in a minute," I promised Father. "I'd just like to wait for a few moments more."

Father nodded in understanding, and then he left.

I waited there for a long time. I waited

CHAPTER
Fifteen

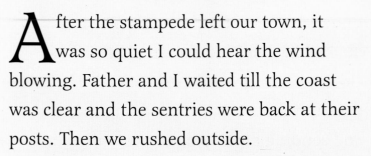

After the stampede left our town, it was so quiet I could hear the wind blowing. Father and I waited till the coast was clear and the sentries were back at their posts. Then we rushed outside.

Lots of prairie dogs were gathered in clumps, talking about the stampede. We didn't want to talk to anyone. We just wanted to find Mother.

It took most of the afternoon, but Father finally found her. She

73

had been hurt in the stampede, and Father had to help her home. It was hard to imagine that Mother, who was so cautious, had been caught away from home.

The only safety that she had found was under the base of some rocks. She had ducked in there and flattened herself as closely to the ground as she could. The cattle passed right over her, dislodging the rock and sending dust flying in every direction.

By some miracle, Mother had not been stepped on. But rocks and sand had struck her again and again. She had lain there, frightened, as the stampede passed over her.

When it finally was over, she didn't even have the strength to get home. We were all so thankful that Father had found her. We tucked her into bed and stood around her, trying to help all at once.

Mother smiled at our help. She looked

at all of us and sighed happily.

"I hope you all know how much I love you," she said. And then she fell sound asleep.

I crept out of the room with the others. I was glad to be a part of my family. We had worked together during some tough times, and we'd always pulled through.

I did some thinking then. All of a sudden, the not-so-good choices I'd made in the past didn't make much sense now. Why had I been so eager to bend the rules? Why didn't I do a better job of listening to Mother and Father? I felt lucky now to have another chance. This was my chance to be the best I could be!

I was through with being a troublemaker. In fact, I wanted to train to be a sentry. If we had more sentries, fewer prairie dogs would get hurt like Mother.

I was going to talk to Father right away.
I couldn't wait to tell him my good news!

BETHANY BACKYARD®

PICTURE BOOKS

by Beverly Lewis
Annika's Secret Wish
Cows in the House
Just Like Mama

by Janette Oke
I Wonder...Did Jesus Have a Pet Lamb?

by Elspeth Campbell Murphy
Is It Christmas Yet, God?

REBUS PICTURE BOOKS

by Christine Tangvald

Christmas Is...For Me!
Easter Is...For Me!

Jesus Is...For Me!
Prayer Is...For Me!

NONFICTION

by Larry Christenson
The Wonderful Way Babies Are Made

by Dave and Neta Jackson
Hero Tales: Volumes I-IV

by Calvin Miller
The Book of Jesus for Families

by B. J. Reinhard
Glow-in-the-Dark Fish and 59 More Ways to See God Through His Creation

Our Place in Space and 59 More Ways to See God Through His Creation

From Bethany House Publishers

Series for Beginning Readers*

YOUNG COUSINS MYSTERIES™
by Elspeth Campbell Murphy

Rib-tickling mysteries just for beginning readers—with Timothy, Titus, and Sarah-Jane from the THREE COUSINS DETECTIVE CLUB®.

WATCH OUT FOR JOEL!
by Sigmund Brouwer

Seven-year-old Joel is always getting into scrapes—despite his older brother, Ricky, always being told, "Watch out for Joel!"

* (ages 6-8)

Series for Young Readers†

THE CUL-DE-SAC KIDS
by Beverly Lewis

Each story in this lighthearted series features the hilarious antics and predicaments of nine endearing boys and girls who live on Blossom Hill Lane.

JANETTE OKE'S ANIMAL FRIENDS
by Janette Oke

Endearing creatures from the farm, forest, and zoo discover their place in God's world through various struggles, mishaps, and adventures.

THREE COUSINS DETECTIVE CLUB®
by Elspeth Campbell Murphy

Famous detective cousins Timothy, Titus, and Sarah-Jane learn compelling Scripture-based truths while finding—and solving—intriguing mysteries.

† (ages 7-10)

04B